A Note to Parents and Caregivers:

Read-it! Readers are for children who are just starting on the amazing road to reading. These beautiful books support both the acquisition of reading skills and the love of books.

 The PURPLE LEVEL presents basic topics and objects using high frequency words and simple language patterns.

 The RED LEVEL presents familiar topics using common words and repeating sentence patterns.

 The BLUE LEVEL presents new ideas using a larger vocabulary and varied sentence structure.

 The YELLOW LEVEL presents more challenging ideas, a broad vocabulary, and wide variety in sentence structure.

 The GREEN LEVEL presents more complex ideas, an extended vocabulary range, and expanded language structures.

 The ORANGE LEVEL presents a wide range of ideas and concepts using challenging vocabulary and complex language structures.

When sharing a book with your child, read in short stretches, pausing often to talk about the pictures. Have your child turn the pages and point to the pictures and familiar words. And be sure to reread favorite stories or parts of stories.

There is no right or wrong way to share books with children. Find time to read with your child, and pass on the legacy of literacy.

Adria F. Klein, Ph.D.
Professor Emeritus
California State University
San Bernardino, California

Editor: Christianne Jones
Designer: Nathan Gassman
Creative Director: Keith Griffin
Editorial Director: Carol Jones
Managing Editor: Catherine Neitge
The illustrations in this book were created digitally.

Picture Window Books
5115 Excelsior Boulevard
Suite 232
Minneapolis, MN 55416
877-845-8392
www.picturewindowbooks.com

Printed in the United States of America.

Library of Congress Cataloging-in-Publication Data
Dahl, Michael.
The tall, tall slide / by Michael Dahl ; illustrated by Sara Gray.
p. cm. — (Read-it! readers)
Summary: On a hot summer day, Tina is too afraid to go down a big slide at the
swimming pool until some new friends offer their help.
ISBN 1-4048-1186-9 (hard cover)
[1. Fear—Fiction. 2. Swimming pools—Fiction.] I. Gray, Sara, ill. II. Title. III. Series.

PZ7.D15134Tal 2005
[E]—dc22
                                                    2005003900

The Tall, Tall Slide

by Michael Dahl
illustrated by Sara Gray

Special thanks to our advisers for their expertise:

Adria F. Klein, Ph.D.
Professor Emeritus, California State University
San Bernardino, California

Susan Kesselring, M.A.
Literacy Educator
Rosemount–Apple Valley–Eagan (Minnesota) School District

PICTURE WINDOW BOOKS
Minneapolis, Minnesota

"Hot! Hot! I'm too hot," said Tina.

4

The hot summer sun baked the neighborhood.

Tina was hot, sweaty,
and sticky.

Tina sat in front of a breezy fan.

She rubbed ice cubes
on her feet.

She ate tons of ice cream. Nothing helped.

11

"I hate being hot!" shouted Tina.

12

"Go and play in the pool," said Tina's father. "The water will cool you off."

Tina looked at the pool.

A tall, tall slide stood next to the pool.

Tina started to climb the tall, tall slide. It did not seem like fun to Tina.

She seemed to be miles above the ground.

The pool looked far, far away.

"I can't slide down there," said Tina.
"I don't care how hot I am."

Tina tried to climb down the stairs, but other kids were climbing up.

"Hi," said a girl. "Aren't you going to slide down into the pool?"

"No," said Tina. "I was just leaving."

"Why don't you go down with me and my friend?" asked the girl.

"OK. That doesn't seem as scary," Tina said.

25

Tina and her new friends made a train.

They zoomed down the slide into the pool.

28

SPLASH!

29

"What did you think of the tall,
tall slide?" asked the girl.

"Cool!" said Tina.

More *Read-it!* Readers

Bright pictures and fun stories help you practice your reading skills. Look for more books at your level.

The Best Snowman by Margaret Nash

Bill's Baggy Pants by Susan Gates

Cleo and Leo by Anne Cassidy

Fable's Whistle by Michael Dahl

Felix on the Move by Maeve Friel

I Am in Charge of Me by Dana Meachen Rau

Jasper and Jess by Anne Cassidy

The Lazy Scarecrow by Jillian Powell

Let's Share by Dana Meachen Rau

Little Joe's Big Race by Andy Blackford

The Little Star by Deborah Nash

Meg Takes a Walk by Susan Blackaby

The Naughty Puppy by Jillian Powell

Selfish Sophie by Damian Kelleher

Looking for a specific title or level? A complete list of *Read-it!* Readers is available on our Web site:
www.picturewindowbooks.com